Wild Cameron Women

Story by Maureen Hull
Illustrations by Judith Christine Mills

Stoddart
Kids
Toronto • New York

I would like to acknowledge with thanks,
Professor Ken Nilsen of the Celtic Studies Program
at St. Frances Xavier University, for his assistance
with the Gaelic phrases in the book.
— M.H.

Published in Canada in 2000 by
Stoddart Kids,
a division of Stoddart Publishing Co. Limited
34 Lesmill Road
Toronto, ON M3B 2T6
Tel (416) 445-3333 FAX (416) 445-5967
E-mail Customer.Service@ccmailgw.genpub.com

Published in the United States in 2000 by
Stoddart Kids,
a division of Stoddart Publishing Co. Limited
180 Varick Street, 9th Floor
New York, New York 10014
Toll free 1-800-805-1083
E-mail gdsinc@genpub.com

Distributed in Canada by
General Distribution Services
325 Humber College Blvd.,
Toronto, ON M9W 7C3
Tel (416) 213-1919 FAX (416) 213-1917
E-mail Customer.Service@ccmailgw.genpub.com

Distributed in the United States by
General Distribution Services
85 River Rock Drive, Suite 202
Buffalo, New York 14207
Toll free 1-800-805-1083
E-mail gdsinc@genpub.com

Canadian Cataloguing in Publication Data

Hull, Maureen, 1949–
Wild Cameron women

ISBN 0-7737-3219-5

I. Mills, Judith. II. Title.

PS 8565.U542W54 2000   jC813'.54   C99-932567-1
PZ7.H84Wi 2000

A resourceful grandmother uses ingenuity and family background
to help her grandchild vanquish nighttime terrors.

THE CANADA COUNCIL | LE CONSEIL DES ARTS
FOR THE ARTS | DU CANADA
SINCE 1957 | DEPUIS 1957

We acknowledge for their financial support of our
publishing program the Canada Council, the Ontario Arts
Council, and the Government of Canada through the
Book Publishing Industry Development Program (BPIDP).

Printed and bound in Hong Kong, China
by Book Art Inc., Toronto

Kate had a problem with bears. They came out of her closet in the night and woke her. They opened their big, red mouths and gnashed their teeth.

"No bears in here," said her father.

"They run away when they hear you coming," explained Kate.

"Go to sleep," her father said.

"I'm trying," said Kate. "It's not easy."

Kate's mother phoned Kate's Nana Cameron.

"She wakes us up every night," her mother said.

"The bears wake us up," said Kate.

"No one can get any sleep," her mother told Nana. "We're all exhausted!"

"I think I'll take a nap on the sofa," said Kate.

"Hmmm," said Nana. "Bears, you say. I have an idea. Let me get back to you."

"Nana thinks she might be able to help," Kate's mother said.

"Good," yawned Kate. "I'm tired of being tired."

A week later, Nana came to visit. She unpacked
three new nightgowns for Kate. Flannelette. Bright
red plaid.

"I made these from the Cameron tartan," said Nana.
"I have a story to go with them."

"What about the bears?" asked Kate.

"Wait for the story," said Nana.

It was a long time until bedtime. Kate didn't think
tartan nightgowns would scare away bears. She was
worried.

"Relax," said Nana. "Let's go to the museum."

Kate and Nana took the bus downtown. They went to the museum to look at bats and bugs. They stopped for afternoon tea at their favorite tearoom next to the museum. Kate had milk tea and Nana had regular. They each had an oatmeal cookie, and then they took the bus back home.

Almost before Kate knew it, it was bedtime.

"Uh-oh," said Kate.

"Not to worry," said Nana. "Wash your face, brush your teeth, put on a Cameron nightgown and I'll tell you the story of the Wild Cameron Women."

"Who?" asked Kate.

"Hurry up," said Nana.

Kate got into bed wearing her bright tartan nightgown. Nana came in and sat beside her.

"Over two hundred years ago," she began, "our ancestors came to this country from Scotland. They wanted a new home where they could make their own music, speak their own Gaelic language, and wear this Cameron tartan. In those days, back in Scotland, they weren't allowed to do such things."

"That's terrible," said Kate.

"It certainly was," said Nana.

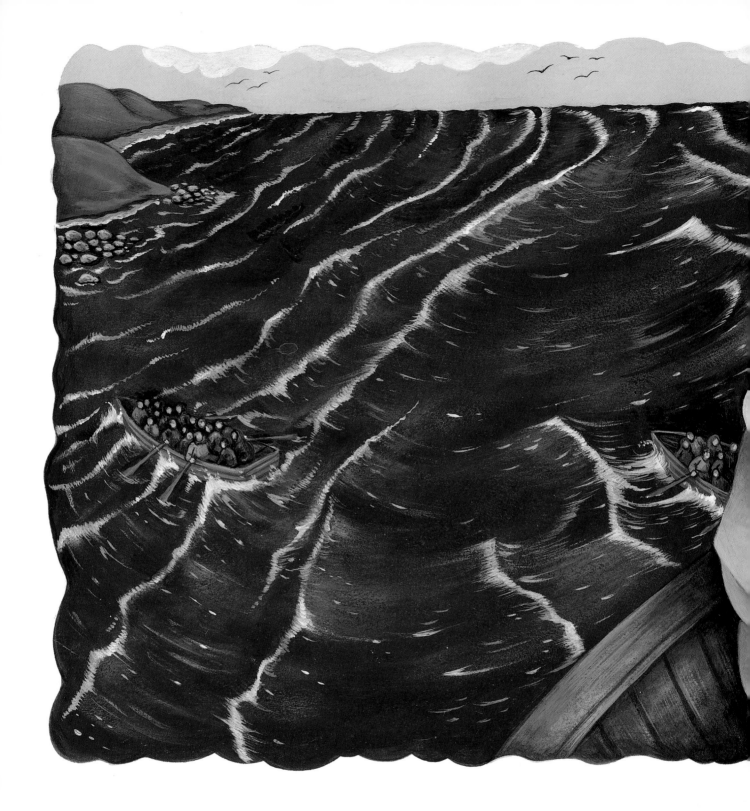

"Your great-great-great-great-great-great-great Nana Kate
Cameron sailed over from Scotland with her husband, Colin."

"She has my name," said Kate.

"There are several Kates in our family," said Nana. "We like it,
so we use it a lot."

"Did she look like me?" asked Kate.

"I think she did," said Nana. "The story says that she was bonnie — that means pretty — with long, flaming red hair and sky-blue eyes. She could run like the wind and she was very brave."

"Yup," said Kate. "That's me."

"Colin and Kate made a farm in the forest. It was very hard work clearing the land for fields. Twice a year, Colin went to town for supplies. It took two days to get there and two days to come home again. Kate stayed at the farm with the kids."

"I bet she wanted to go to town too," said Kate.

"She did later," said Nana, "when the children were big enough to stay by themselves."

"I could stay by myself," said Kate.

"Anyway, Colin went to town. Kate and their two children stayed home. The oldest, Fergus, was two. The baby, Katie Margaret, was seven months old."

"Another Kate," said Kate.

"Katie Margaret was asleep and Fergus was playing in the cabin. Their mother took two buckets and went to the creek to get some water. While she was gone, Fergus unlatched the door and toddled outside. A large, cranky bear came out of the forest and headed straight for Fergus."

"Oh, no!" said Kate, hiding her head under the blankets. "He's going to eat Fergus!"

"Well, Fergus grew up to be your six-greats grandpa, so he didn't get eaten," said Nana.

"Whew!" Kate uncovered her head.

"Your seven-greats Kate heard the bear growl and came running."

"She could run like the wind," said Kate.

"She could and she did. She ran straight at the bear, yelling at
the top of her lungs, *Falbh as-a-seo, a bhéist mhosach!*"

"What?" said Kate.

"You say it like this," said Nana, speaking very slowly. "*Fa-luv
ass-uh-shoh, uh vaysht vossukh!* It's Gaelic for 'Get out of here,
evil beast!'"

"Did the bear eat Kate instead?" asked Kate.

"Just imagine what he saw," answered Nana. "Kate was yelling at the top of her lungs. Her flaming red hair and her red tartan skirts were flying. And then she threw the two buckets of icy, cold creek water in his face."

"Ouch," said Kate.

"She scared him silly," said Nana.

"Hooray!" said Kate.

"The bear ran howling back into the forest. Kate grabbed Fergus and ran into the cabin. Then she made herself a cup of tea to settle her nerves."

"Milk tea settles my nerves," said Kate. "Did she give Fergus some?"

"Of course," said Nana, "and an oatmeal cookie. The bear told all the other bears and ever since then they have all been scared of Wild Cameron Women."

"But, Nana — they aren't scared of *me*."

"That's because they don't know you're a Cameron," said Nana.

"Now, go to sleep. When the bears come, sit straight up in bed and yell '*Get out of here evil beast!*' in Gaelic as loud as you can. Wave your arms so they can see your nightgown."

"I think I need a bucket of water," said Kate.

"Good idea," said Nana. They sent Kate's father to the garage for a bucket. He filled it with water and put it beside Kate's bed.

"I need to practice throwing it," said Kate.

"Maybe not," said Nana. "They just need to see it."

"I'll throw it if I have to," said Kate.

"Oh, dear," said her mother.

"Only if I have to," promised Kate.

Kate fell asleep. Her mother, father, and nana went to bed and fell asleep. The house was quiet. So quiet you could hear the closet door handle turn. Click.

Kate woke up. It was dark in her room, but she could see the closet door opening. Five bears came out. Carefully, she reached for the lamp switch. Just as they were beginning to open their horrible red mouths, she snapped on the light, sat up in bed, shook her sleeves, and yelled.

It was pandemonium!

The bears all tried to jump out the window at once. Kate hopped up and down on her bed, yelling in Gaelic. Her nana, mother, and father came running. By the time they got to Kate's room, the bears were gone.

"They jumped out the window," she told them.

Her father stuck his head out and looked up and down the street. "I don't see any bears."

"Of course not," said Nana. "You don't think they'd stick around, do you? They're so scared, they're halfway to Timbuktu."

"Three-quarters," said Kate.

There were bears in Kate's room for a few more nights after that. By the third night, she didn't even bother to sit up. She just waved one red tartan arm in the air. The bears ran like sixty. By the end of the week, all the bears in the world had heard that Kate was a Wild Cameron Woman.

Not one would go near her house again. Her father took the
bucket back to the garage.

"I didn't get to throw it," sighed Kate.

"Thank goodness," said her mother.

Kate still wore the nightgowns, though. She was wearing one on the last night of Nana's visit.

"They feel cosy," she said when Nana came to tuck her in. "And they match my flaming red hair."

"*Oidhche mhath!*" Nana whispered.

"Say it slowly," yawned Kate.

"*Oy-hyuh vah,*" said Nana, as she kissed Kate. "It means, 'Good night.'"